Disney

Bibbidi Bobbidi Academy

Rory and the Magical Mix-Ups

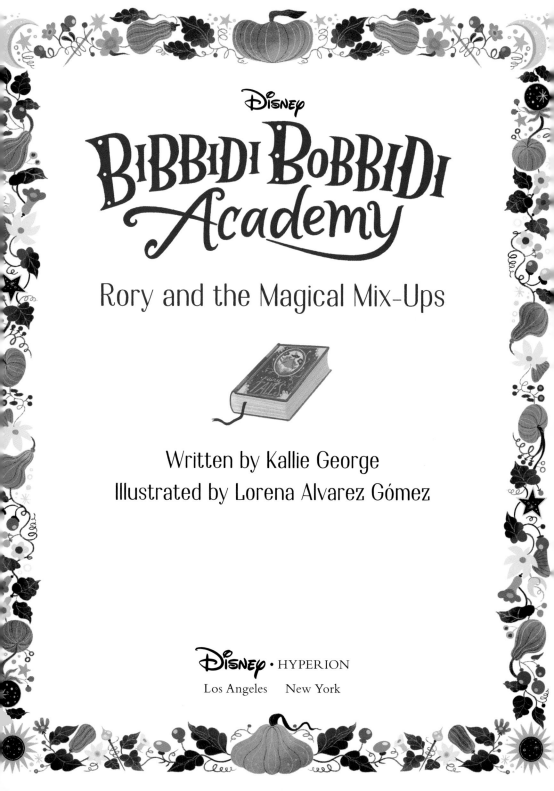

DISNEP

BIBBIDI BOBBIDI Academy

Rory and the Magical Mix-Ups

Written by Kallie George

Illustrated by Lorena Alvarez Gómez

DISNEP • HYPERION

Los Angeles   New York

First Hardcover Edition, October 2022
First Paperback Edition, October 2022
1 3 5 7 9 10 8 6 4 2
FAC-004510-22238
Printed in the United States of America

Library of Congress Control Number: 2021950243
Hardcover ISBN 978-1-368-05739-4
Paperback ISBN 978-1-368-06655-6
Visit www.DisneyBooks.com

To all children who struggle with spelling. I did too.

—K.G.

To my sister Liliana.

—L.A.G.

Bibbidi Bobbidi Academy

CHAPTER 1
Rory Spellington

Rory Spellington could spell all sorts of words.

Like *fairy*. *F-A-I-R-Y*. (She was a fairy herself.)

And *wish*. *W-I-S-H*. (She loved wishes.)

She could even spell the word *magic*. *M-A-G-I-C*. (Magic is tricky to spell. Still, Rory could do it.)

But when it came to *magical* spelling . . .

That was a problem.

Rory always mixed things up. What she wanted to spell with her wand and what came out of her wand never matched.

When she wanted socks, she got rocks.

Instead of her hair,
her brush combed
a chair.

And when she
tried to spell
some juice, her
wand made a
goose!

3

Her mom and dad said magic was all about practice. Rory hadn't practiced much. Although she was a fairy, and her parents were too, they didn't live with the other fairies.

They lived in disguise in a non-magical town.

So Rory hadn't gone to Pumpkin Preschool or done Summer Sparkle Studies like most fairies. She had played in parks and had gone to camps with children. But now it was time to start school.

Rory wanted to be a fairy godmother, so here she was at the Bibbidi Bobbidi Academy, the boarding school for fairy godparents-in-training.

At least, she was *almost* there.

The path was steep. Her suitcase was heavy. It would be nice to give her suitcase wings. She waved her wand. She said the magic words. She knew those. "Bibbidi Bobbidi Boo."

But . . . instead of wings, her suitcase started to sing.

La-la-la-la!

"Shhh," shushed Rory.

"LA-LA-LA-LA!" her suitcase sang louder.

She clasped it shut and began to carry it up the hill.

How embarrassing. At least she was going to the right place. At school Rory would learn how to spell with magic.

Except, where WAS the school? All she could see was a giant . . . pumpkin?

CHAPTER 2
The Academy

Around the pumpkin, fairies of all sorts and sizes fluttered and floated. One was even a merfairy! Rory was excited, and just a little nervous.

The Fairy Godmother, the school's headmistress, was there too. The very fairy who had helped Princess Cinderella!

"Welcome, my dears!" she exclaimed. "I'm so pleased to see you here.

"Well, well, no time to delay. To your class, students. Be on your way."

Everyone stared at the pumpkin, confused.

"Oops!" The Fairy Godmother chuckled. "I almost forgot. Now, for the magic words. Bibbidi Bobbidi Boo!" She waved her wand.

POOF!

The pumpkin grew . . . into a
beautiful school! It had a sparkly
green tower and windows framed
by silver vines.

"Oh, it's wonderful," said Rory. "If only I could spell like that."

"*I* already can," said a fairy near her, with a toss of her hair. "See? I will make this seed into a pumpkin." The fairy picked up a pumpkin seed and said the magic words.

Pop!

The seed turned into a pickle. "Well, it's *practically* the same thing."

It wasn't.

Still, Rory was impressed.

"That's Tatia. She has to be first at everything," a very sparkly fairy whispered. "My name is Mai. Mai Magicwhisp."

"I'm Rory Spellington," said Rory.

She didn't have a chance to say more, because the Fairy Godmother continued with a wink, "Soon you will all be able to do big magic. Now . . . with a wave of my stick, to finish this trick . . . Bibbidi Bobbidi BOO!"

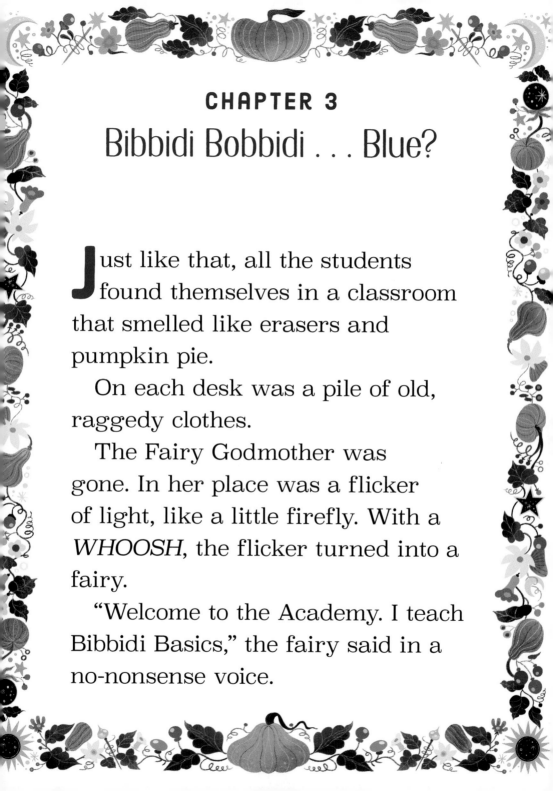

CHAPTER 3
Bibbidi Bobbidi . . . Blue?

Just like that, all the students found themselves in a classroom that smelled like erasers and pumpkin pie.

On each desk was a pile of old, raggedy clothes.

The Fairy Godmother was gone. In her place was a flicker of light, like a little firefly. With a *WHOOSH*, the flicker turned into a fairy.

"Welcome to the Academy. I teach Bibbidi Basics," the fairy said in a no-nonsense voice.

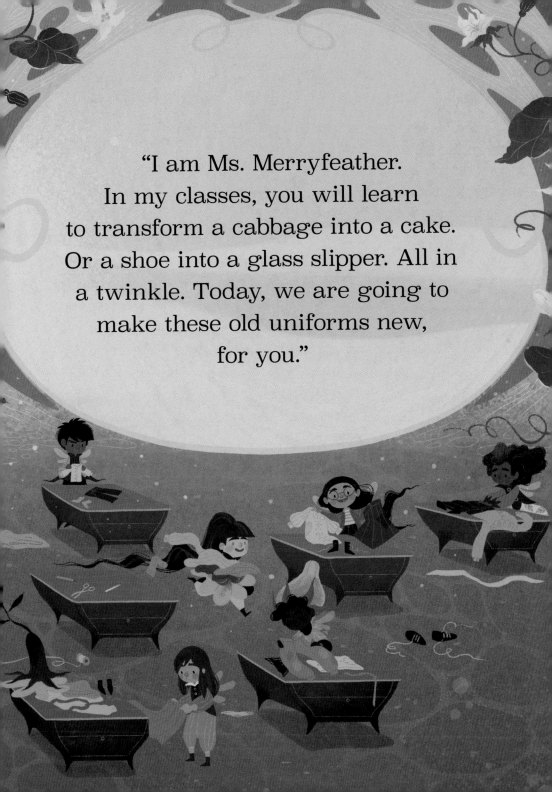

"I am Ms. Merryfeather.
In my classes, you will learn
to transform a cabbage into a cake.
Or a shoe into a glass slipper. All in
a twinkle. Today, we are going to
make these old uniforms new,
for you."

At her command,
the students lifted
their wands.
Tatia went first.

Poof!

Perfect.

Mai was next.

Poof!

Perfect, with sparkles.

18

The merfairy,
who was named
Ophelia, waved
her wand.

Poof!

Her clothes slipped
right over her tail.

And Cyrus, one of
the fairy-godfathers-
in-training, added a
bow with a star in the middle.

Finally, it was Rory's turn. She waved her wand. She thought *new*. She said the magic words.

But . . . Uh-oh!

POOF!

Instead of new, Rory made the uniform blue! And not just the uniform . . . All the clothes!

The walls!

Even the ceiling!

Only Rory's cheeks weren't blue. They were bright red.

Ms. Merryfeather did not look impressed.

With a brisk Bibbidi Bobbidi Boo, she cleaned up the mess—and fixed Rory's uniform.

"As we say, you have to work your way up to miracles. With a little practice and hard work, by the end of the week, you will all be ready for your first magical assignment."

Magical assignment? wondered Rory.

Everyone else raised their wands to ask questions.

But . . .

BRIIIINNG!

The school clock chimed.

"That's all for now," said
Ms. Merryfeather. "The Fairy
Godmother will tell you more
later. Time to tuck your wands
away."

Rory did, with a sigh. It was
still blue. But she didn't say
anything.

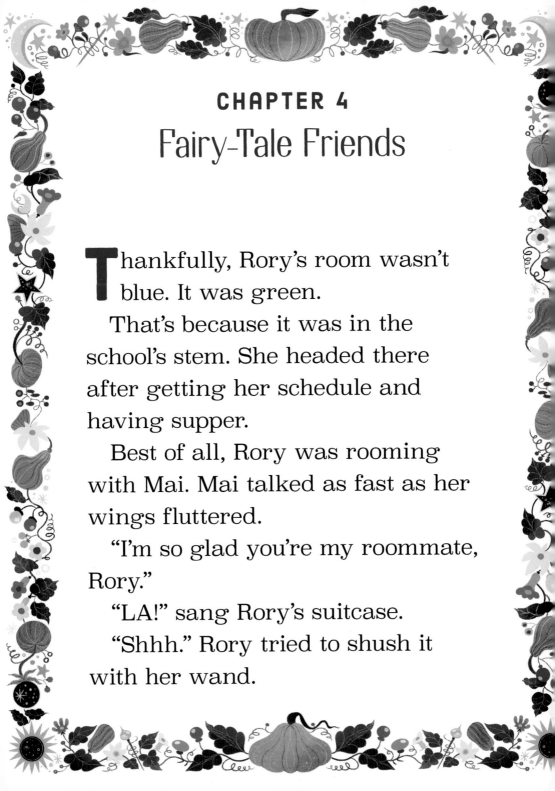

CHAPTER 4
Fairy-Tale Friends

Thankfully, Rory's room wasn't blue. It was green.

That's because it was in the school's stem. She headed there after getting her schedule and having supper.

Best of all, Rory was rooming with Mai. Mai talked as fast as her wings fluttered.

"I'm so glad you're my roommate, Rory."

"LA!" sang Rory's suitcase.

"Shhh." Rory tried to shush it with her wand.

La-la-la-la!

"Ooh, is your wand blue?" Mai said. "My wand needs something more, but I'm just not sure what. More *is* my motto, you know."

"LA!" sang Rory's suitcase again.

"Here. Let me," said Mai. She waved her wand.

The suitcase stopped.

"Wow!" said Rory.

"I'm good with suitcases," explained Mai. She DID have a whole sparkly stack. As they changed into their pj's, Mai continued, "I wonder what our magical assignment will be? I can't wait to find out. And we have Reverse Curse class in the morning! I can't wait for that either. I'm too excited to fall asleep!"

Reverse Curse class. How could Rory reverse a curse if she couldn't even spell? Now Rory couldn't sleep either.

But she knew what to do: R-E-A-D. Read. She pulled a book out from her suitcase. It was big with fancy letters.

"Ooh. What's *that*?" asked Mai.

"A fairy-tale book," explained Rory. "My parents run a bookshop and are fairy-tale writers. They went to Bibbidi Bobbidi Academy, like us. But they decided to write about wishes coming true. I want to grant actual wishes, though."

"Me too!" said Mai.

Rory smiled. "Sometimes reading stories before bed can help you fall asleep. I could read one, if you'd like?"

Mai nodded—more than once. They snuggled under their cabbage-leaf covers, and Rory began.

Reading worked like a charm.

CHAPTER 5
A Froggity Fog

The next morning, though, Rory's spelling troubles started again. The first thing Mr. Frog, the curse-breaking teacher, asked was for everyone to take out their wands.

Rory did, trying to keep positive. Still, she couldn't help but notice some fairies looking at her nervously.

Mr. Frog sat on a chair shaped like a lily pad. Around the classroom were snoring, snorting pigs.

"Always keep your magic wands at the—*ribbit*—ready," Mr. Frog croaked in a gloomy voice. "You never know when a curse might hit. I was a perfectly happy frog until I met that mean wizard. Now I'm stuck as a human."

One of the pigs snorted.

"Most curses can be broken, though," Mr. Frog continued. "These hogs accidentally ate some sleeping apples and became volunteers for today's class. I want you to wake them back up. Just think, *Wake up, hog*."

Tatia waved her wand. One hog woke up. "I did it *Snort!* first!" she said.

Snort! Another hog woke up. Actually, two did. That was Cyrus. He seemed very good at spelling.

Wake up, hog, thought Rory. *Wake up, hog*.

She waved her wand. "Bibbidi Bobbidi Boo." But . . .

33

Oh no! Not again!

Instead of waking up a hog, she woke up a . . . FOG!

It rolled out of her wand . . .

and filled the room . . .

and spilled into the hall.

It was as thick as a blanket. Rory couldn't see, but she could hear some voices.

"How lovely and damp," croaked Mr. Frog. "It reminds me of home."

"It reminds me of morning swims beside the shore," Ophelia said quietly.

"It reminds me of flying in the rain. Storms are scary, but I like fog," said Cyrus.

It reminded Rory of something too.

"One time at camp the fog was so thick we all played hide-and-seek," she said.

"What's that?" asked Mai.

"You hide, and someone tries to find you," Rory explained.

"What fun! Let's play!" said Mai.

"Yes! Yes!" came the reply. Even Mr. Frog joined in.

Soon they were all playing and
taking turns finding one another.

Rory felt a lot better about her magical mix-up. Until she heard another voice. It was Tatia's.

"That Rory is nothing but trouble. Let me be the first to say, she will never complete our magical assignment. She will never grant a child's wish. *Never.*"

CHAPTER 6
Wand Charms

Tatia's words swirled in Rory's head like a fog.

Even when the *real* fog was lifted and all the hogs were woken up.

After lunch, Rory curled up in her room and read the spelling book Mr. Frog had given to her to practice.

But her wings kept fluttering. It was hard to focus.

Was Tatia right? Would they really be granting a wish? Rory wanted to do that more than anything, but you had to be able to spell to grant a wish.

Rory would definitely fail the assignment and be sent home.

She tried to make her suitcase sing again to help her feel better.

This time she made string.

At least string was useful.

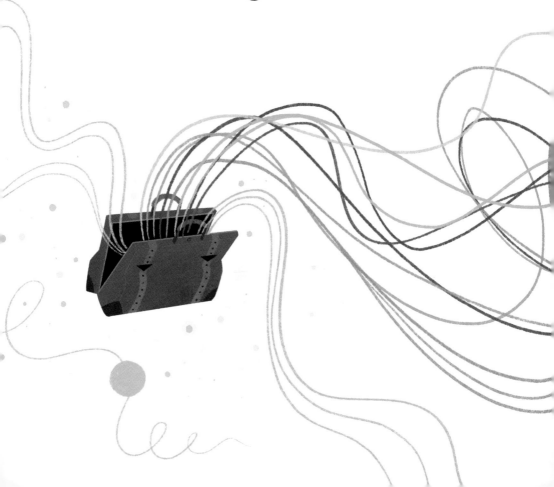

She could transform it without magic. She saw Mai's wand on her bed.

That gave her an idea. Mai had complained about her plain wand.

Rory knew just what to do: B-R-A-I-D. Braid. She'd make Mai something special.

She finished just as Mai flittered in.

"What's that?" asked Mai. "It looks pretty."

Rory was proud of it. She had even added a charm, a star, from one of her bookmarks.

"It's a friendship bracelet,"
explained Rory. "Kids make them
for each other. I made this one for
you. You wear it . . ."

"Like this?" Mai put it on her
head like a crown.

Rory giggled. "Actually, children put them around their wrists, but I thought you could tie this around your wand."

"OOH!" Mai said. She tied it to the tip and waved. "It's more than magical! Can I make one for you?"

Rory smiled. "I'd love that," she said.

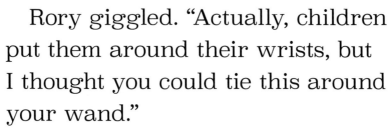

CHAPTER 7
The Wish Bubbles

As the days went on, Rory practiced her spells a lot. And got better . . . a little. Luckily, there were no more big disasters.

Plus, not all of Rory's classes taught spells. In Princess History class, run by Ms. Ebony, a retired witch, they read stories. Rory was great at that. She was fine at Flying Lessons too. And Twinkle Time, where you learned how to make an entrance.

But her favorite class was Wish
Whispering, when you listened for
the wishes children made on stars.

Rory tried not to think about the magical assignment.

Much.

But then the day arrived.

"Today you're with me, and what a class this will be," said the Fairy Godmother, floating at the front of the classroom. "It's your first magical assignment. To grant a child's wish. So you can use what you know and give it a go."

Rory gulped.

They really WERE granting wishes!

"I knew it," said Tatia. "My older sister told me. She graduated from Bibbidi top of her class!"

The Fairy Godmother pulled out a wand that Rory had never seen. It was SO long the tip skimmed the classroom ceiling. It had a hoop on the end.

"This is
the thingamabob
that does the
job," said the Fairy
Godmother. "A Wish Wand.
It makes wish bubbles. When
you pop one, you will go where
you are needed. Then, with a
swish, you can grant the wish."

"But . . ." protested Rory.

"Goodness, yes. It's *lovely*,
isn't it?"

"But . . ." Rory tried again.

"I know, my dear. Hurry up,
you say!"

The Fairy Godmother waved the
wand. "Bibbidi Bobbidi Boo."

Bubbles floated down.

Cyrus and Ophelia each touched a bubble. *POP!* They were gone. *Pop! Pop! Pop!* Other fairies disappeared.

Rory didn't want to touch a bubble.

Too late . . . An enormous bubble touched her!

And Mai and Tatia, too!   POP!

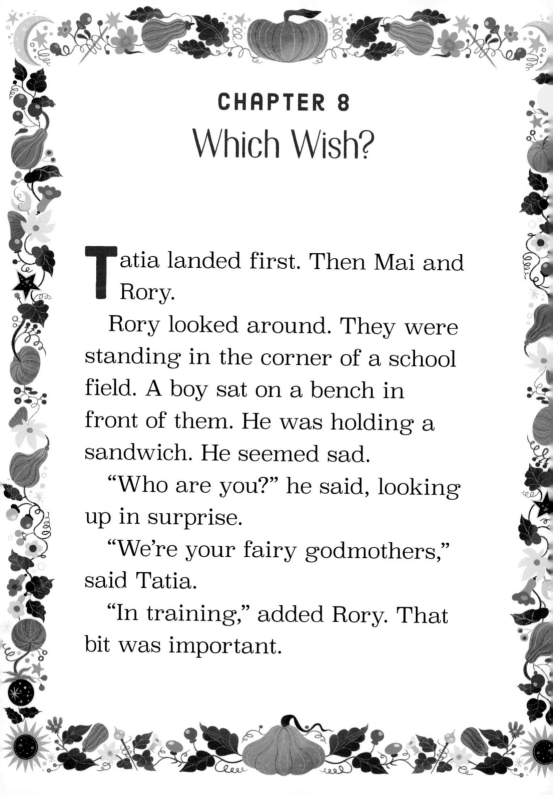

CHAPTER 8
Which Wish?

Tatia landed first. Then Mai and Rory.

Rory looked around. They were standing in the corner of a school field. A boy sat on a bench in front of them. He was holding a sandwich. He seemed sad.

"Who are you?" he said, looking up in surprise.

"We're your fairy godmothers," said Tatia.

"In training," added Rory. That bit was important.

The boy blinked. "I must be dreaming."

"No!" piped Mai. "It's true. We're here to grant your wish. What is it?"

In a small voice, the boy said, "If you really were fairy godmothers, you would know."

The fairies gave each other worried glances. None of their teachers had told them what to do if this happened.

Tatia spoke first.

"I know what your wish is. That cake is really plain looking. Everyone likes a cake with icing." She waved her wand.

"Wait," started Rory. She knew it was a sandwich, not a cake. But . . .

Poof!

The boy frowned.

Mai took out her wand next. "I know. That crown doesn't even sparkle! You must wish it was fancier."

"Wait . . ." started Rory. She knew it was just a baseball cap, not a crown.

But . . .

Poof!

The boy's frown grew.

"I was sure that was it," Mai said with a sigh. "Maybe I can add something more . . ."

"No, I know what the wish is *now!*" said Tatia. "It's obvious. He doesn't need a fancy crown if there's no party to go to." With a wave . . .

Poof!

"Everyone wants a birthday party," said Tatia smugly.

Or maybe not.

Because, instead of smiling, the boy started to cry!

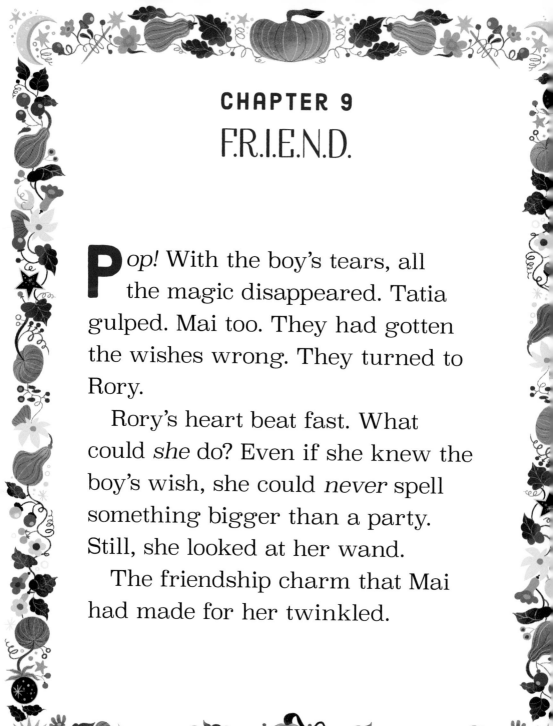

CHAPTER 9
F.R.I.E.N.D.

Pop! With the boy's tears, all the magic disappeared. Tatia gulped. Mai too. They had gotten the wishes wrong. They turned to Rory.

Rory's heart beat fast. What could *she* do? Even if she knew the boy's wish, she could *never* spell something bigger than a party. Still, she looked at her wand.

The friendship charm that Mai had made for her twinkled.

Of course. *F-R-I-E-N-D*. Friend.

The boy was sitting all alone.

She sat down beside him. "Is your wish to have a friend?"

The boy nodded. "I . . . I just moved. I had to leave everyone behind. I don't have anyone to sit with. Or play with."

"It's okay. I can help," said Rory. But how?

Rory took a deep breath. She had figured out the wish without magic.

Maybe she didn't need magic right now either.

After all, she hadn't needed it to help fall asleep, or to decorate a wand, or to have fun in the fog. Or even to make a friend herself.

She saw a girl on the swings who was alone too. Rory had an idea. She waved her wand. But not to cast a spell. To cut the boy's sandwich in two.

"Take half to that girl on the swings," suggested Rory.

"But . . ." stammered the boy.

"Trust me," said Rory. "You can do it."

The boy gulped but nodded.

Rory gulped too.

Would it work?

Rory, Mai, and Tatia watched and waited.

It did!

Just as Rory had hoped.

Soon, the boy and girl were sharing, swinging . . . smiling.

And the moment the boy laughed . . .

POP!

In a shower of sparkles, the fairies returned to school.

CHAPTER 10
Ice Cream Stream

Back in the classroom, the other students and the Fairy Godmother were waiting for them.

"Wow!" said Tatia. "I'm sorry I was so mean before. Let me be the first to say, you were amazing."

"More than amazing," said Mai. "You really know children."

Rory beamed.

The Fairy Godmother was beaming too.

"Good job, Rory. Good job, everyone. You don't always need a swish to grant a wish." She gave Rory a wink. "But right now, a Bibbidi Bobbidi Boo is just what to do."

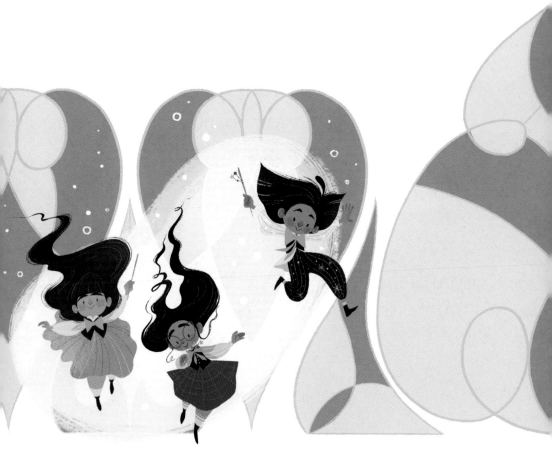

With that, the headmistress lifted
her wand again.

"*More* wish bubbles already?"
said Rory.

"Oh, no, dear. No more dreams to
fulfill today. . . ."

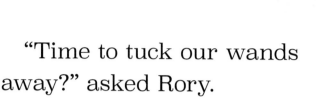

"Time to tuck our wands away?" asked Rory.

"Oh, no, dear. Not that either." Her eyes twinkled. "Time for us to eat and play!"

Whoosh!

Not bubbles, but streamers burst from her wand.

How nice! Soon, everyone started to celebrate the end of their first week.

And when the Fairy Godmother asked them to make some ice cream, enough to fill a glass, Rory took a deep breath. "Let me try."

She waved her wand. She said
the magic words. And . . .

POOF!

She DID make ice cream.
But it didn't just fill a glass. It
filled their ENTIRE class!
Y-U-M! Yum.